Clams All Year

by
Maryann
Cocca-
Leffler

Boyds Mills Press

Published by Caroline House
Boyds Mills Press, Inc.
A Highlights Company
815 Church Street
Honesdale, Pennsylvania 18431
Printed in Mexico

Publisher Cataloging-in-Publication Data
Cocca-Leffler, Maryann.
    Clams all year / Maryann Cocca-Leffler.—1st ed.
[32]p. : col. ill. ; cm.
Summary : A large extended family spends the summer together every
year at the ocean, and one year a bumper crop of clams provides meals
well into the following winter.
ISBN 1-56397-469-X
1. Clams—Fiction—Juvenile literature. 2. Seashore—Fiction—Juvenile
literature. [1. Clams—Fiction. 2. Seashore—Fiction.] I. Title.
    [E]—dc20   1996   AC
Library of Congress Catalog Card Number 95-79097

First edition, 1996
Book designed by Amy Drinker, Aster Designs
The text of this book is set in 18-point Souvenir.
The illustrations are done in gouache and colored pencils
on watercolor paper.

10 9 8 7 6 5 4 3 2

In memory of my grandfather,
Emanuel Vivilecchia
1893-1989

❖

And to all the
Coccas and Vivilecchias
who still enjoy summers
at the Hull House

"**I'll** wake you up at five o'clock,"
Grandpa said as we got ready for bed.
"The tide will be low at 5:13."
"Okay, Grandpa," everyone said as
we kissed him good night.

Tomorrow we'll be going
clam digging with Grandpa...
again.

My brothers, my sister, my cousins, and I
all spend summers together in a large,
rambling house on the ocean in New England.

For three days straight, we had been
getting up at sunrise to dig for clams.
Grandpa taught us how to find clams
with our feet— when you see bubbles,
you dig like crazy.

So far we haven't had too much luck.

On Sunday all eight of us went digging.
We only found three clams.

On Monday we found a bunch of starfish,
but no clams.

On Tuesday, only six of us got up.
We found four clams and two
pieces of sea glass.

That night there was a big storm.
The thunder and lightning
kept us up half the night.

Early the next morning, when it was still dark,
Grandpa called to us.

Eight of us sleep in two rooms in the attic,
the boys' room and the girls' room.
I woke Carmen up, but the others
were too sleepy to come.

We crept out of the house as the sun
peeked over the horizon.
Grandpa carried his favorite pitchfork
and metal pail.

We followed him onto the deserted beach.
The tide was very low.
It seemed to take forever to get to the water.
The storm had littered the shore with
seaweed and shells.

We started feeling with our feet.
Suddenly, there were bubbles everywhere.
Grandpa dug quickly with his pitchfork.
We dug with our shovels.
CLAMS!
Soon our pails were full.
It was a bumper crop.

Carmen lugged the two
overflowing pails back to the house.
He yelled from the backyard.
"Everybody up! We need help!
The beach is loaded with clams!"

Soon a parade of people marched
out the back door, still sleepy-eyed.
They were armed with pails
and shovels and sacks and pans—
anything they could think of to carry clams.
They even dragged my baby brother's
plastic pool to the beach.

Everyone dug.
It seemed like we were finding a clam every second.
By seven o'clock all the containers we had
were overflowing with clams!

My grandpa spent the whole day sitting in the hot sun cleaning the clams. My mother and aunt helped him.

Our job was to rinse out the best shells and let them dry.
Later we could use them to make baked stuffed clams.

That night we had clams for dinner:
clam chowder, baked stuffed clams,
and spaghetti with clam sauce!

My mom and my aunt spent the rest of the
evening washing and freezing the clam meat—
all twenty-five pounds of it.

We ate a lot of clams that summer. In fact, we had clams all year—clams at our Labor Day cookout…

clams at Thanksgiving dinner....

We even had baked stuffed
clams on Christmas Eve!

And as we ate,

we laughed about that warm summer
morning when we found our
bumper crop of clams!